Liam the Lion

An Inspirational Story of a Boy's Struggles
and His Path to Swimming Victory!

Nick Baker

Olympic Coach
Founder of Peak Performance Swim Camp

Liam the Lion

An Inspirational Story of a Boy's Struggles and His Path to Swimming Victory!

Published by Positive Swimming

www.swimcamp.com

Book design by:

Brian Adams PhotoGraphics, www.brianadamsphoto.com

Cover illustration by:

Natalya Pilavci

Printed in the United States of America

Liam the Lion

An Inspirational Story of a Boy's Struggles and His Path to Swimming Victory!

Nick Baker

1. Title 2. Author 3. Swimming

Nick Baker's full collection of books are available on swimcamp.com and Amazon:

- *101 Winning Ways*
- *The Swimming Triangle*
- *Un-Limit Yourself!*
- *In The Know*
- *Are You Worth It?*
- *Mind Body Skill*
- *Liam the Lion*

About the Author

Nick Baker has spent the past 56 years of his life pursuing his passion. First, as a swimmer where he qualified for the Olympic Trials, second as an Olympic Coach, and third as the founder of Peak Performance Swim Camp. His coaching philosophy is unique, believing that success in the pool begins with a swimmer's "inner excellence," and as it improves, so does the other. He's a master at artful communication, leaving no stone unturned to convey his winning message. His latest book, *Liam the Lion*, will inspire you to tackle your journey with courage and resolve.

Contents

Year One

It was the fall of 1992, and I had just returned from the Olympic Games where my swimmer, Lisa Flood, reached the semi-finals in the 100-breaststroke. It was a tremendously exciting time in my life as I had finally achieved my lifelong ambition to become an Olympic coach. But reality had sunk in, and I was now back in the real world running team tryouts. The turnout was overwhelming thanks to the hype that surrounded the Olympics. In fact, so many people showed up that a line formed outside the building! One by one, swimmers shuffled onto the pool deck for their one shot. Those who showed promise made the team. Otherwise, it was up to me to break the bad news to them as gently as possible, something I found very difficult to do.

As the morning dragged on, I could sense the tension building in those still waiting their turn. I ran out of time due to the enormous turnout, so I offered a second tryout the following Saturday. As I packed up to leave for the day, I heard someone say, "Hey coach, what about me?" When I turned around, I saw a short, chubby boy age fourteen or so, standing next to the starting block. His name was Liam, and he told me that he loved swimming and was desperate to make the team. I liked his spunk, so I agreed to give him a chance. The moment he pushed off the wall, I knew he wasn't up to the task. His butterfly, if you could call it that, was a train wreck! He zigged and zagged down the pool in the backstroke, and squirmed like a worm in freestyle. Only his breaststroke showed a spark of potential. Compared to the other 13 and 14-year-old boys on my team, he didn't stand a chance. Breaking the bad news to him would not be easy, but I had no other choice.

As I began to speak, I sensed that he already knew the verdict; at which point, he interrupted me and said, "Coach, please give me a chance. I love swimming, and it's the only thing that really matters to me. I'll do anything you ask if you give me a chance." By now, tears were welling up in his eyes, and his face turned red as a beet. I soon found myself in a very tough predicament. My brain told me that he wasn't good enough and that he'd be a drag on the team, but my heart told me to be a better man and put the desperate needs of a young 14-year-old boy first. So I paused for a moment, stared straight into his eyes, and said, "Okay, you want a chance? I'll give you one, but you better be willing to back it up with action and give one hundred percent." With that, his face burst into an immense smile as if he'd won the lottery. We then shook hands and made it official. Unfortunately, I wasn't sharing Liam's enthusiasm because I knew it would be an uphill battle for both of us. I told him that practice started a week from Monday and we then parted ways. In the meantime, I still hadn't recovered from my whirlwind Olympic experience in Barcelona. I spent the final days of my vacation doing what I enjoyed most, walking my beloved dogs, Rudy and Hanna.

When I arrived on deck for the first practice of the season, there was excitement in the air much like the first day of school, and I saw many familiar faces including Liam's. There he was grinning ear to ear and wearing a tiny red and white pinstripe Speedo that was way too small for his chubby body.

After a brief team meeting outlining my expectations for the year, we started warming up with Liam at the very back of Lane 1, the slowest of six lanes. Everything was running smoothly, except you guessed it, Lane 1! Liam was swimming straight down the middle, smashing into everyone, and creating a real safety hazard. I quickly ran over to him and shouted, "Stop!" at the top of my lungs. He screeched to a halt and looked at me with a stunned look on his face. I explained the swimming rules of the road to him, which marked the beginning of the many "Liam lessons" to follow.

Autumn was a magical time for me because of the cooler temperatures and the brightly colored leaves. As the weeks passed, I could see significant improvement in all of my swimmers, including Liam. Although not pretty to watch, he was making positive strides and had now moved up to the third spot in Lane 1. It looked like he was a man of his word. His butterfly, backstroke, and freestyle were still very rough, to put it mildly, but his breaststroke definitely showed signs of promise. I'd arranged a dual meet the following weekend with a local swim team and was eager to see my group in action. Surprisingly, they swam well beyond my expectations, and I could tell that my "no garbage yardage" approach to training was indeed paying off. To establish a benchmark, I'd entered Liam in the four 100s - butterfly, backstroke, breaststroke, and freestyle. I'm stunned to this day that I remember his butterfly race, as I vowed to erase it from my memory bank! The first length was somewhat recognizable, but the last 75 was a horror show. And his backstroke and freestyle races resembled a man walking on stilts in the circus. To my surprise, Liam looked pretty good in the breaststroke and actually won his heat! His teammates cheered him on throughout the race, giving him a much-needed boost of confidence.

We attended several other competitions over the next few months. As a whole, we were swimming at around ninety percent best times, and there was a vibe of success in the air. It was a golden moment for me, as I could feel my swimmers growing in proficiency, confidence, and stature. I was expanding Liam's event portfolio, but always made sure to enter him in the 100-breaststroke, his favorite and best event. He continued to improve in all of his strokes and was starting to flirt with finals in the breaststroke. Liam was a quiet person and accepted any success he attained humbly and gratefully, and I always made sure to recognize his accomplishments.

It was now the middle of December, and our annual Christmas Classic Invitational was about to get underway. My swimmers were bursting with anticipation, and Liam too had a sparkle in his eye. As expected, we dominated the meet, which was a huge morale booster for all. On average, we had three to four swimmers in every final! Liam also made finals for his first time, and although he was pleased with his preliminary performance, it was a different story that night. He looked terrified in the warm-up, moving through the water like a robot. The first 50 of his race looked terrific, but the rest was a complete disaster, and Liam finished dead last and well behind the pack. Upon touching the wall, he quickly jumped out of the pool and ran into the locker room. I waited for him to come out, but he never did; I sent a teammate in after him, but Liam was long gone. He failed to show up for the next day of competition which I found very troubling.

My swimmers returned to practice the following week superpsyched, but sadly Liam never showed up. We then took a short, well-deserved break to enjoy the spirit of Christmas before the start of our annual winter training camp. Liam was missing in action which alarmed me, so I called his mother Ruth, and learned that her husband was gravely ill. She asked if she could drop by the pool later that week to chat and I agreed. Upon meeting, I asked her about Liam, and a tear came to her eye. Sadly, he was having a difficult time dealing with his father's long-term illness, which was declining by the week.

To make matters worse, Liam was being picked on at school. Ruth had spoken to the principal, but to no avail. To avoid conflict, Liam would wait after school until everyone had left for the day before running home at full speed. He would also lock himself in his room and seldom went outside on the weekends. Ruth was incredibly proud of the strides Liam had made in swimming and desperately wanted him back in the pool. I promised her that I would do everything in my power to make that happen.

It was the last day of the year, and we'd just finished the final practice of training camp. I packed up my car and drove over to Liam's house, who had agreed to have breakfast with me with some prodding from his mother. When I arrived, he was standing on the veranda with a sad look on his face. I'd seen that look before, and it was never a good sign. We then drove off for a bite to eat. When we sat down, I sensed Liam was fearful of what I might say. Thus, I began by telling him that I wasn't there to judge him, but instead to help him. He looked somewhat relieved and began to let down his guard. I went on to explain that swimming was a journey with many twists and turns, and that his disappointing performance at the Christmas Classic was unfortunate but not surprising, as every swimmer experiences setbacks especially the unseasoned ones. Liam began to sniffle but regained his composure. He then proclaimed how unfair life was, but I quickly shot back, telling him that life isn't fair and that success has nothing to do with the fairness of life. I then shared a little secret with him, how I had been bullied for many years, and how it had destroyed my self-worth.

As I continued, Liam's eyes grew as large as dinner plates, as if he was in a trance. I went on to say that I had grown up with a target on my back and that everyone in school picked on me. They said terrible things, threw rocks, tripped me, and spit on me. They even tore my shirt off and flushed it down the toilet! He was curious to learn how it affected me, and I told him that it made me fearful of everything. It also made me a choker, making it impossible for me to swim fast under pressure. My confession shocked Liam as he saw me as the fearless leader. I explained to him that I hadn't always been filled with courage, but had learned to become that way later in life. I'd decided I was sick and tired of being pushed around and wanted desperately to be the person that God had intended me to be. With tears in his eyes, Liam opened up and began to share his stories about being bullied and the fear that ensued. I seized the moment, telling him that we had something in common, and that I could help him overcome his fears if he were willing to try.

Over the following months, the positive change that took place in Liam was remarkable. He became a top trainer and performed admirably in competition. We grew closer together as we saw each other as "bully buddies." He worked to the max in practice and feared nothing. To honor his courage, his teammates gave him the nickname of Liam the Lion!

O ur summer championship meet was only two weeks away as we began our final taper in preparation. My swimmers were raring to go, and they did not disappoint. We achieved all best times with many making finals. Liam the Lion also lived up to his name dropping four full seconds in the 100-breaststroke! Upon realizing his time, he jumped out of the pool like a kangaroo and ran over to me, shouting, "Coach, I did it! I beat the bullies!" He walked on air for the rest of the weekend, achieving best times in his other events as well. What a way to cap off the summer!

When the season ended, I gave my swimmers a well-deserved break, as it fulfilled three needs. One, it gave them a chance to rest physically after months of intense training. Two, it gave them a mental break from the "go, go, go world of competitive swimming." Three, it offered them an opportunity to live a "normal" life, albeit a short one. Unfortunately, that wasn't the case for me, as I had been selected to coach at an all-star event, an opportunity that I couldn't pass up. I was okay with it though, as I had given up living a typical life some twenty-two years prior, when I first began coaching. All I needed was one week or so, to spend some quality time with my two best buddies, Rudy and Hanna.

It was late August, and I decided to organize a last-minute mini training camp to jump-start our short course season. Everyone showed up, except for one. You guessed it,

Liam was nowhere to be found. I thought it was highly unusual as he had ended the season on an all-time high. The next day, I decided to call Ruth to find out more. Sadly, the news was devastating as Liam's father had taken a turn for the worse and was now on his deathbed! A feeling of sadness overtook me as I thought of my beloved father, who had died of cancer after many years of struggle and suffering. I remembered how lost and confused I felt and wondered how Liam would handle it. Two nights later, his father passed away in his sleep. His family held a vigil in his honor which I attended. Liam was there, sullen and sad. His body appeared lifeless as he sat next to his mother firmly clutching her hand. I immediately went over to them to pay my respects and to express my sympathy, before sitting down to pray in the nearby chapel. Three weeks would pass before I saw Liam again.

Year Two

A new swim season was officially underway. Last year had been our best ever with so much to be thankful for. This year could be even better as eleven of my swimmers were on the verge of qualifying for elite-level competitions. I knew it was possible if we worked harder and smarter. To build team unity, I organized an outing at a local pizzeria, and everyone attended including Liam! He received a royal welcome, and it was great to have him back in the fold.

The first day of practice was nerve-racking as swimmers eagerly awaited their new lane assignments. Based on last year's performance, Liam was given the number one spot in Lane 3. His teammates applauded when they heard the news, but Liam looked shocked! As they readied for warm-up, he stood off to the side, and I went over to him and asked, "Are you okay?" He replied, "Yes, but are you sure you want me to lead off Lane 3?" "Absolutely," I said. I went on to say that I wasn't giving him this opportunity because I liked him more than the other kids or felt sorry for him, but rather because he earned it fair and square. At that point, a glow of confidence appeared on Liam's face, and I knew I'd made the right decision. Little did we both know, but he was in for a wild ride!

Lane leaders enjoyed a special status on my team, but at a price, as they were expected to be an example to others. They could never hold back, because if they did, they'd hold back the other swimmers. All of them knew what I expected of them, and Liam was no exception. Over the months to follow Liam the Lion lead with courage and became a shining example to all.

My training curriculum was delivering the results I'd hoped for, and over the months to follow, three of my swimmers qualified for Senior Nationals and five for Junior Nationals. Unfortunately, Liam didn't make the grade but inched ever closer. By now he'd become a dominant leader within the group and admired by all, not just for his courage and work ethic, but for his kindheartedness and humility. Physically, he began to muscle up, but he still had a hint of baby fat around his mid-section.

As we headed into spring, it was time to turn our clocks ahead, giving us more time to enjoy the great outdoors. It was a beautiful springlike evening when I received a call that would turn my world and Liam's world upside down. Ruth was on the phone, and she was sobbing heavily. She explained that Liam had been trail riding with his friends that afternoon when he fell off his bike and fractured his right arm. Oh my God,

I thought, he's the most unlucky guy in the world, and can't catch a break no matter how hard he tries.

After Monday's practice, I drove over to Liam's house to see how he was doing. When I walked into the living room, I found him sitting on the couch, looking downcast and depressed. "Are you okay?" I asked, but he didn't respond. I walked over and sat next to him, and asked a second time, "Are you okay?" But he just sat there and stared at the floor.

I could tell that he'd been crying because his eyes were red and his cheeks tearstained. I wrapped my arm around his shoulder and said, "Look, I know that life has been tough on you with those bullies and your father's death, but your swimming has been looking up, and I believe it's only a matter of time before you hit the jackpot." At that, he pointed to his cast and said, "I'm not winning any jackpots with this arm." He then walked out to the veranda with me close behind and screamed, "Life's not fair, life's not fair! I've tried so hard, but bad things keep happening to me. Why me, why me?" I didn't have an answer for him, because there wasn't one. Life isn't fair, but to succeed, one must have the courage to persist no matter what. How is it fair that people go hungry, that animals are abused, and that close friends betray you? Unfairness is everywhere, a reality of life; but even so, one must endure through hardship to be victorious in the end and there's no other way. Before leaving, I made Liam promise that he'd come to practice the next day, and thankfully he did. His teammates were thrilled to see him and eager to autograph his cast. Fortunately, his fracture was minor, and the doctor felt he'd be back to his old self in six weeks or so. If only that were the case.

*S*adly, I had to move Liam back to Lane 1 due to his injury. At first, he took it in stride and spent the bulk of his practice time performing drill and kick sets. I had experience working with injured swimmers, and knew that the most important thing was to keep them motivated and feeling productive. Liam made visible gains in the first few weeks, but after that I noticed a change in his behavior. He started to show up late for practice and barely broke a sweat. I was somewhat prepared for this, but continued to hope that I could keep him moving forward until his fracture healed, and he could resume training at full tilt. We competed in a few competitions without Liam, and I knew that it was affecting his morale. The poor guy, he didn't fracture his arm on purpose, but he was indeed paying for it now. I did my best to cheer him up, but to no avail. On occasion, I'd remind him of the hundred percent promise that he made to me long ago, but it had lost its meaning by now. Liam began to miss practice frequently, and when he was there, he acted like he didn't want to be. I felt I was losing the battle, but I was determined to save the day.

Finally, six weeks had passed, and the cast was removed, thank God! Liam began taking physical therapy and was able to return to full training two weeks later. Although it had been a rough road, it seemed like the worst was behind us. I had to remind him to take it easy for fear that he would injure his arm a second time, but his drive to make up for lost time was immense. Two weeks later, the doctor gave Liam the green light to compete, but I wasn't prepared for what would happen next.

Coaching in the Great White North is a hardship due to the cold winter months, but you can't beat the northern springtime. It was now early May, and we moved outside to a 50-meter pool located a few miles outside of town. The pool was far more spacious, which created a better training environment for all. Long course is definitely more challenging than short course, and it took my swimmers time to adjust. We put in some solid training as we prepared for our first long course meet of the season. To be cautious, I only entered Liam into the 50-freestyle, the 100-freestyle, and the 100-breaststroke.

In the 50-freestyle, Liam added two seconds to his converted time. He slapped the water in frustration, ripped off his cap, then disappeared into the locker room. His second swim, the 100-breaststroke, was a full five seconds slower. This time he banged his fist on the wall before heading into the locker room. There was a part of me that wanted to rush to his aid, but I felt it was finally time for him to deal with his setbacks on his own. When it came time for the 100-freestyle, Liam was missing in action. I later learned that he'd left the building and walked home by himself, a distance of more than four miles! His behavior agitated me, especially given the amount of time, effort, and patience I'd dedicated to his comeback; but I let it go and refocused my energies on my other swimmers. Unfortunately, Liam didn't return to practice on Monday or the days to follow, and his teammates didn't see or hear from him either.

B y now the summer season was heating up, and I had little time to spend getting Liam back on track. I called him numerous times and left messages, but he never returned my calls. His swimming had come to a screeching halt; however, the rest of my group was swimming up a storm. The swim year had finally come to an end, and it was time for a well-deserved break. I heard nothing from Liam, but hoped he'd moved on from his disappointing experience.

It was now September, and I was gearing up for another successful year of swimming. Things were hectic to say the least, and my phone was ringing off the hook, while my answering machine was experiencing a nuclear meltdown. One day, as I played back my messages, I noticed that someone kept calling and hanging up, and I wondered who it was and why they were being so persistent. The next morning the phone rang at 6:30, early for some, but not for a swim coach. When I answered, there was dead silence. Then I heard, "Coach Nick, this is Liam, and I wanted to talk to you about coming back to swimming. Do you have time to talk now?" I was somewhat shocked and replied, "Liam, it's great to hear your voice. I thought you had moved to another planet." "No," he said. "I've just been dealing with a lot of stuff, and I think I finally sorted it out. I'd love to sit down and talk if you have the time." I replied, "I'd like that, so let's meet for lunch tomorrow."

When we met the next day, Liam had a guilty look on his face, and I could sense he was extremely uneasy. Before I could say a word, he blurted out, "I want to apologize for my behavior. I was very immature and disrespectful, and I didn't know how to handle my anger, so I ran." "No worries," I replied. "I've dealt with this kind of behavior many times before, and it's nothing new." I continued by saying, "We learn more about ourselves through the tough times and I think you learned a lot about yourself this past summer. Wouldn't you agree?" He answered, "Yes, I do, and the biggest thing I learned is that success doesn't happen overnight. You must be patient and keep working hard no matter what." "You sound like an old sage," I said. Liam chuckled and said, "Do you think I have a chance of swimming in college one day? My mother and I are struggling since my father passed away, and I can't afford to go unless I get some financial assistance." I responded by saying, "There's no guarantee, but I believe it's possible, especially in the breaststroke." Liam looked at me and said, "How do you know that?" Then I proceeded to tell him my favorite farmer story.

A family went to an orchard one day to pick some apples. When they arrived, they saw an old farmer sitting on his porch in a rocking chair. They approached and said, "Good morning, old farmer, we'd like to pick some tasty apples from your beautiful orchard." The farmer replied, "You're more than welcome, but you'd better hurry before it starts to rain." The father laughed and said, "No need to worry about that because the weatherman says it will be clear and sunny all day." The farmer paused and replied, "That may be well and good, but the rain is still going to fall so you'd better get picking." The father seemed amused by the old farmer and said, "So you think you know more than the weatherman?" To which the farmer replied, "Maybe not, but I have my own way of telling. I listen to the birds, watch the leaves turn in the trees, and smell the air, and that's all I need to know." With that, the rain poured.

Liam looked at me as if I had lost my mind. "Coach Nick, what do apples have to do with me swimming in college?" I went on to tell him that I was like the old farmer and could predict his swimming future based on my many years of swimming and coaching experience. I assured him that he had excellent potential and even predicted he'd be voted team captain one day. That was all he needed to hear.

Year Three

I t was the fall of 1994, and I was eager to get the new swim year up and running. Liam the Lion, true to his nickname, got off to a roaring start. Practices were now much harder than ever before. I pushed him day and night, yet he never backed down. Physically, he was now a beast and could easily do 50 pull-ups without stopping, and his impressive strength turbocharged his swimming. At our annual Christmas Classic, Liam shocked the field by winning gold in both breaststroke events. Two weeks later, he placed second in the 200-breaststroke behind the fastest swimmer in the country and made his Junior National cut! Five of his fellow teammates also qualified, so it was a tremendous short course season all around. My holistic training approach was paying off, and I was eager to see what the future held.

Liam was now six feet tall, and his height and strength gave him a huge competitive advantage. He was all-consumed by his breaststroke technique, swimming each length of practice with purpose. He continued to be a leader in training, and his confidence grew stronger by the day.

Overall, things were running smoother than ever, and I was incredibly proud of my swimmers and the progress they had made thus far. All I needed to do was keep them moving in a forward direction, but that was easier said than done!

It was mid-March when I received a phone call from Mr. Bell, a fitness trainer at Liam's high school. I could tell by his voice that something was seriously wrong! It turns out that Liam was showing off in the weight room and pulled a muscle in his lower back. What an idiot I thought, as he was swimming faster than ever before. Back injuries are the most concerning and must be treated with extreme caution. As a result, Liam spent the next ten days in rehab and out of the pool! Missing that amount of practice time at the peak of the season could prove to be disastrous, and I wondered if Liam had the maturity and inner strength to bounce back.

When Liam finally returned to practice, I could tell that he had lost his edge. His body looked flabby, his stroke looked sloppy, and he seemed a little shell shocked. I wasn't surprised because that's what happens when swimmers spend too much time out of the water. We didn't have time to waste as summer Junior Nationals were only a few months away, and Liam needed to be in tip-top shape well before then. I scoured my brain in hopes of coming up with something that would get him back on track in a hurry.

I called Liam into my office the next day and told him about an 85-year-old swimmer named Charlie, who I'd known for several years. He was a legend in the local swimming community who swam 3,000 meters a day, seven days a week! But that wasn't the most unique part of his story. He'd also undergone two hip replacements, two shoulder replacements, and a heart triple bypass - yet he never let it stop him or slow him down. Swimming was his life, and nothing mattered more than that! I then asked Liam, "Other than your family, what's the most important thing in your life?" "Swimming," he replied. Then I went on to say that if he loved it that much, he'd use Charlie's story as a source of inspiration. Two weeks later, Liam was back to his old self. Thank God for small miracles! That summer I gave him a short taper before heading off to Junior Nationals, as he had missed ten days of training in the spring. It was now time for Liam to deliver.

On the morning of the 100-breast-stroke, Liam woke up with a sore throat and slight fever; yet another setback for him, but hopefully not a major one. His morning performance was solid, all things considered, qualifying sixth in the semifinals. When we met at the warm-down pool, things seemed off. Liam told me that he felt achy and wanted to go back to the hotel and sleep, so I gave him some chicken soup and he went off to bed. When we met in the hotel lobby later that afternoon, he looked zombie-like, not a good sign to be sure. Liam finished dead last but did not react negatively. Wow, what a relief, I thought. He was silent on our walk back to the hotel, and I could sense his disappointment. I put my chaperone in charge of Liam and begged her to perform a miracle.

The big day had finally arrived, and Liam was in excellent spirits and looking much better healthwise. His 200-breaststroke preliminary time was a personal best, qualifying fourth in the semifinals. Overall, a pretty amazing feat, considering that two days prior he was on his sickbed. When I reviewed Liam's race, he assured me that he could swim much faster that night. Even though I was anxious for him, I didn't let it show, and prayed that he wouldn't crash and burn. Liam was up against some stiff competition, and I knew it would be his biggest challenge ever. At the 150-meter mark, he was in fourth place, but on the final 50, he blew past the field and touched the wall first! What a swim, what a win.

When we boarded the plane for our return trip home, Liam was flying high in more ways than one. All he could talk about was the upcoming short course season and his goal to make the Olympic Trials.

He planned to take a short break and com-mence dry-land training on his own. Wow, talk about a man on a mission!

Year Four

I t was 1996, the Olympic year, and there was a buzz of excitement in the air. From experience, I knew this would be a banner year for us. I was incredibly proud of our many accomplishments and was eager for more. It had been a team effort with plenty of help from my assistant coaches, my volunteer parents, and most of all, the Almighty One.

B y this point, I had seven swimmers who qualified for the Olympic Trials. Hopefully, I could add a few more. It wouldn't be easy as the time standards were super fast, and we were running out of time. It would be a big test for me as a coach, but deep down inside, I knew I could do it. Liam was now the top dog in Lane 4 and training with unbridled passion. From the first day of practice, he had two goals in mind - to make the Olympic Trials and to swim in college - and he knew that one would lead to the other. The Trials were in early March, and it was now late September.

My swimmers were extraordinarily committed and sacrificed daily. By this point, their lives centered around school and swimming, with little time left for fun outside of the pool. I had tremendous respect for them and committed myself to helping them achieve their goals. I spent hours a day planning to ensure that I advantaged my swimmers to the fullest. Workout by workout, I pushed them to the limit and focused on the smallest of details, which annoyed them to no end.

By late November, we were training and competing better than ever, but I felt there was still more to do. I began videotaping our practice sessions and discovered that my swimmers were slow on and off the walls. As a result, I made turn technique a top priority. It paid off in a big way, as we were now out-turning our competition.

It was now mid-February, and anticipation ran high as we geared up for our state championships, our last big meet before the Olympic Trials. A lot was riding on the outcome, especially for Liam, who had caught the attention of numerous college coaches. While swimming in college is the goal of almost every competitive swimmer, only a handful ever make it. It's a demanding endeavor that requires academic and swimming excellence. Liam was an outstanding student, so I had little concern there, but his biggest hurdle was his inconsistency in competition. Over the past three years, his results were up and down like an elevator, and that had to stop!

I t was day one of States with Liam swimming the 100-breaststroke. His morning performance was one second faster than his best time, a good beginning for sure! Finals were even better as he dropped another full second, but he was still shy of his illusive Trial cut. Although somewhat disappointed, Liam took it in stride and moved on.

T he next morning in prelims, Liam the Lion roared, posting a personal best time in the 200-breaststroke and only four-tenths of a second off the cut! While frustrating, we both knew that he had what it took to make it at finals that night. Liam and I walked back to the hotel together and talked about everything else except swimming. It was a beautiful day outside, and life was good, but would it stay that way?

Liam's make-or-break breaststroke final had arrived. When he mounted the block, I noticed something very unusual. He was wearing a different pair of goggles, an unwise move to say the least. It's always best to stick with the ones you know, especially with so much at stake. Liam blasted off the block true to form, and broke out a full body length ahead of the field, but his stroke looked choppy. I wondered what was going on, until I realized his goggles had filled with water and he couldn't see where he was going! What a dummy, I thought. How could this be happening on the most important day of his swimming career? Sadly, Liam placed fifth in finals, well off his best time. He jumped out of the pool and disappeared into the locker room, just like the old days, only this time I followed. I found him slumped over a bench looking like he'd just received the death penalty. I went over to him and said, "Liam, why did you switch goggles?" He sobbingly replied, "My mother bought them for me and told me that they would bring me good luck." I replied, "That was very kind of her, but you should have worn them in practice first to figure out the proper fit." Even though it was a boneheaded move on his part, there was nothing more we could do. At that moment, reality set in and Liam realized he had blown his chances, and perhaps jeopardized his college future. Wow, what a letdown, and what a way to end the season!

L iam left the pool without saying goodbye, as he'd done many times in the past. But this time it felt as if his quest had come to a screeching halt! One part of me felt very sad for him, the poor guy, I thought, as I recalled the first time that we'd met and how far he'd come. His personal life and swimming life had been a roller coaster ride with more downs than ups - between the bullies, his father's passing, and the numerous other setbacks he had experienced. In my mind, Liam was a winner in every way, shape, and form, and his swimming journey deserved a winning ending.

I looked into running a time trial once we got back to our home pool, but it would take too long to get approval. I then called every coach I knew, and some I didn't, in hopes of finding one more chance for Liam to swim his 200-breaststroke. However, I kept coming up empty, and time was running out! Two days later, I received a phone call that would save the day. There was a last chance swim meet the following weekend, and we were welcome to attend. I called Liam with the fabulous news, and he was so excited that he dropped the phone, smashing it to bits!

The following week, Liam focused on his technique while keeping his muscles in race-ready form. Through trial and error, he knew what he needed to do to swim fast. His teammates showed up to train with him and offer their moral support, and

I knew that Liam was mentally, technically, and physically prepared for the big day. Everything seemed in order, but knowing him, I was never quite sure.

R ace day was upon us, and Liam was primed and ready to go. Even though it was just a time trial, the entire team showed up to cheer him on, a moving experience to say the least. All at once they began to chant, "Liam the Lion, Liam the Lion, Liam the Lion!" When he mounted the block, the pool went silent. Like always, he blasted off the block like a rocket ship and proceeded to swim his fastest 50 ever! It concerned me as I feared he might have gone out too fast. At the 100-mark, Liam's time was eight-tenths quicker than his best 100-split, but could he hang on? His third 50-split was slightly slower than I hoped for, and it now came down to the final 50. When he touched the wall, we were in shock as Liam had made his Trial cut by six-tenths of a second! From a distance, I could see the pride in his eyes and the weight of the world lift off his shoulders. Liam was now an Olympic Trial Qualifier! News spread like wildfire and in the weeks to follow numerous college coaches contacted him with full scholarship offers! Liam competed in Trials and bettered his time by another two seconds, which was the icing on the cake! Unfortunately, he wasn't fast enough for finals.

After much thought, Liam chose a major college in the Midwest and earned All-American standing four years in a row. He was undefeated in his college conference, and voted team captain in his junior year as I'd predicted! Liam competed in the 2000 Olympic Trials and finished third in the semifinals. All in all, a tremendous achievement, considering the many obstacles he'd overcome! After graduating from college, with a degree in exercise physiology, he became a swim coach and a father of one. His son now swims in his footsteps and is one of the fastest young breaststrokers in the country.

L iam's story is not unique, as every person experiences setbacks along life's journey. It could be a homeless person who once lived a life like yours or mine, or a billionaire who had more money than they could count! No one gets through life without encountering some form of hardship. Liam refused to give in as he followed his passion, dared against overwhelming odds, and persevered until his dream came true. No doubt, he made many mistakes along the way and paid dearly for them, but that's part of the process called life. We must all learn from our mistakes, but continue to advance towards our dream with increased wisdom, confidence, and faith in ourselves. Liam learned the hard way, but came back again and again, and grew stronger each time. Keep Liam's story close to your heart and use it as a source of daily empowerment.

Feel inspired? Join Coach Nick Baker at a Peak Performance Swim Camp event. Year-round swim camps and clinics. Multiple locations worldwide. View camp schedule and details at swimcamp.com.

Made in the USA
Monee, IL
20 December 2019